Get the Picture, Jenny Archer?

by Ellen Conford

Illustrated by Diane Palmisciano

Little, Brown and Company
Boston New York Toronto London

First Edition

The characters and events portrayed in this book are fictitious. Any similarity to real persons, living or dead, is coincidental and not intended by the author.

Library of Congress Cataloging-in-Publication Data

Conford, Ellen.
Get the picture, Jenny Archer? / by Ellen Conford ; illustrated by Diane Palmisciano. — 1st ed.
p. cm.
Summary: Jenny lets her imagination run way with her when she decides to enter a photography contest and starts taking "candied," that is candid, pictures around her neighborhood.
ISBN 0-316-15247-1
[1. Photography — Fiction. 2. Imagination — Fiction. . 3. Humorous stories.] I. Palmisciano, Diane, ill. II. Title.
PZ7.C7593G1 1994
[Fic] — dc20 94-16714

Springboard Books and design is a registered trademark of Little, Brown and Company (Inc.)

10 9 8 7 6 5 4 3 2 1

WOR

Published simultaneously in Canada
by Little, Brown & Company (Canada) Limited

PRINTED IN THE UNITED STATES OF AMERICA

1

Jenny Archer couldn't wait to get to her grandparents' house.

"We have a surprise for you," her grandfather had told her over the phone.

She leaned forward as far as she could in the backseat of the car. The seat belt tugged at her.

"Can't you drive any faster?" she asked her father.

"No," he said.

"We're almost there," said her mother. "You can see the sign already."

Jenny's grandparents had an apartment in Boxwood Gardens. It was a building for older people. Her grandparents lived on the third floor.

"What do you think the surprise could be?" Jenny wondered.

"I don't know," said her mother. "Grandpa didn't tell me."

"Maybe it's a puppy!"

"I don't think it's a puppy," said Mrs. Archer. "You already have a dog."

"It's probably not a pony," Jenny said.

"It better not be," said Mr. Archer.

"I hope it's not underwear," Jenny said.

"I don't think your grandparents would expect you to be excited about underwear," said her father.

"Yeah," said Jenny eagerly. "They give *good* surprises."

They drove into the Boxwood Gardens parking lot.

"I'm going right up the stairs," Jenny said.

Her hand was on the buckle of her seat belt. "I'm not going to wait for the elevator."

"I didn't expect you to," her father answered. "But I hope you'll let me stop the car before you get out of it."

Jenny giggled.

Inside the building, Jenny dashed for the stairs. She reached the third floor before her parents even got on the elevator.

Grandma and Grandpa were waiting at their door. Jenny skidded to a stop in front of them. "How did you know I was here?" she asked.

"We heard you on the stairs," Grandpa said.

"But how did you know it was me?"

"Jenny, this is a building for senior citizens," said her grandmother. "Nobody but you runs up those stairs at sixty miles an hour."

Jenny grinned. "I couldn't wait to see my surprise."

"Don't we even get a kiss?" Grandpa said.

He tried to frown, but his eyes danced.

"Oh, of course!" Jenny threw her arms around him and gave him a loud kiss on the cheek. Then she hugged and kissed her grandmother.

"I couldn't wait to see *you*, too," she said. "It wasn't just the surprise."

The elevator doors opened. Jenny's mother and father got out.

"What took you so long?" Grandpa asked. "Jenny got here hours ago."

Suddenly Jenny saw that Grandpa was holding one hand behind his back.

"What have you got behind your back, Grandpa?" she asked.

"Well," he began, "we've been taking a photography class at adult education."

Jenny nodded.

"So we decided to buy a really good camera," he went on.

Jenny felt a flutter of disappointment. "Is

E-Z Aim 'n' Click

that the surprise? That you bought a new camera?"

"No," said her grandfather. He pulled a box from behind his back. He held it out to Jenny. "This is the surprise. We're giving you our old camera."

"Oh, a camera." Jenny tried to sound excited. But she wasn't, really. She had never especially wanted a camera.

She would be a lot more excited about a pony. Or a puppy. Or a rubber raft.

She smiled as brightly as she could. She tried not to show how disappointed she was.

Oh, well, she told herself. At least it wasn't underwear.

2

"But you can have lots of fun with a camera," her mother told Jenny. "I love taking pictures."

"Maybe they should have given the camera to you," said Jenny. She was sitting cross-legged on the living room floor. Her dog, Barkley, was sleeping with his head in her lap. She was trying to read *Kid Talk* without waking him up.

"This isn't like you, Jenny," said Mr. Archer. "You've always been eager to try new things."

"I guess I expected a more exciting surprise. And it's not really a new thing. It's just a used —"

Jenny stopped in the middle of her sentence. "Look at this!" she shouted.

Barkley's eyes flew open. He gave a little yelp and scrambled to his feet.

"Sorry, Barkley." Jenny held the paper out to her parents. "But look! *Kid Talk* is having a contest. A *photo* contest!"

"You can enter a picture of a person, a place, or a pet," Jenny said. "And you have to think up a clever title for it. I bet I could think up lots of clever titles!"

Her father nodded. "I'm sure you could."

"There's also a prize for the best candied picture," Jenny said. She frowned. "What's a candied picture? A picture of something sweet?"

Her mother laughed. "You mean *candid*."

Jenny pointed to the word. "It says candied."

Her father looked at the paper. "It does say candied."

"It's a mistake," said Jenny's mother. "They

KID TALK

mean candid. That's a picture of someone who doesn't know you're taking a picture."

"Oh," said Jenny. "Wow, look at the prizes! A computer! A mini-TV! A two-year subscription to *Kid Talk*!"

"A year's supply of Skinny Farms fat free yogurt," her father read.

"Well, most of the prizes are good," said Jenny. "I'm going to start taking pictures right away!"

She ran up to her room. She grabbed the camera box and ran back down to the living room. Grandpa had given her two rolls of film with the camera.

He'd helped her load the film. He had shown her how to take pictures.

She hadn't listened very carefully. But the camera was called an E-Z Aim 'n' Click. So it couldn't be too hard.

Jenny pulled the camera out of the box. She held it up to her eye. She looked through the viewfinder.

"This is easy," she said. "There's a green outline and a dot. That shows you where the center is."

"Maybe you ought to read the instruction booklet," her father said.

"Why?" asked Jenny. "All you have to do is aim" — she turned the camera toward her mother — "and click." She pressed the button on top. "Click!" she said.

A little flash of light went off. Her mother blinked. "Jenny! You should have warned me you were taking my picture."

"I wanted a *candied* shot," Jenny said.

Her father laughed. "Click," said Jenny as she snapped a picture of him. "That was a good one."

She heard a whirring sound. "What's that noise?"

"That's the film advancing," her father said. "You know, there are things you should learn about. Even with a simple camera."

"That's right." Mrs. Archer nodded. "There's

more to taking pictures than just aiming and clicking."

"Then why do they call it an E-Z Aim 'n' Click?" Jenny asked.

Her father folded up the booklet. He put it down on the coffee table. "For people like you," he said. "Who don't like to read instructions."

"I'm probably not going to take a prize-winning photo right away," Jenny said. "I know that. This first roll of film is only for practice."

"Well, just have fun with the camera," her mother said. "That's what Grandpa wanted."

"I will," said Jenny. "But I'd better start having fun fast. There are only two weeks left in the contest!"

3

That night Jenny took six pictures of Barkley. Three of them were of Barkley sleeping. "I wish you'd do something more interesting than sleep," Jenny told him.

He yawned. Jenny snapped a picture of him yawning.

"Yawning is a little more interesting than sleeping," Jenny said. "But I don't think it's a prize winner."

She took three pictures of Phyllis, her giant goldfish. She snapped one picture from the side of Phyllis's bowl. Then she stood on a

EZ AIM
-n- click

chair and took one looking down into the bowl.

"I don't know how good these are going to be," Jenny said to Phyllis. "You were moving."

She took a picture of her parents watching television. She took a picture of her father clipping his fingernails.

She went outside onto the front steps. She took a picture of the house across the street. Then she went around back. She took a picture of the trash cans next to the kitchen door.

"Jenny, it's dark," her mother called. "Why are you taking pictures outside?"

Jenny went back into the house. "I took pictures of people," she explained. "And I took pictures of pets. Now I need pictures of places."

"But it's too dark," her mother said.

"The flash worked. Could I dump one of the garbage cans out?" she asked. "My picture would be a lot more interesting with garbage all over the ground."

"No!" her mother said. "What an idea. It's bad enough when the raccoons do it."

Jenny's eyes lit up. "Maybe they'll come tonight!"

"I hope not," Mrs. Archer said.

"But if they do," said Jenny, "don't clean up until I get a picture!"

By nine o'clock, Jenny had used up her first roll of film. "I can't wait to see how my pictures came out," she said.

"I'll drop off the film on my way to work tomorrow," her mother said.

"You took twenty-four pictures already?" her father asked.

"Yes."

"Of what?" he asked.

"People, places, and pets," Jenny answered. "But I'd better think up some really clever titles. I don't think these pictures are going to be very exciting."

4

Jenny was right.

Her pictures weren't very exciting.

Some of them were even terrible.

"Look at this." She showed her mother a picture of Phyllis. All you could see was a white blur.

"It's hard to take a flash picture through glass," Mrs. Archer said.

"And the pictures of Barkley," Jenny said. "He doesn't even look like a dog. He looks like a big blob of licorice."

"Well, he's black," her mother said. "And he's lying on a dark rug. He sort of blends in."

Some of the pictures were fuzzy looking.

"You must have moved the camera," her father said.

"But I've taken pictures with your camera," Jenny said. "They never come out this bad."

"It's a different kind of camera," he said.

"But this one's supposed to be easy," complained Jenny.

"It probably is," said Mr. Archer. "After you read the instructions."

"Oh, all right," grumbled Jenny. "But they shouldn't call it an E-Z Aim 'n' Click if you have to read a whole book before you use it."

The instruction booklet turned out to be more interesting than Jenny expected. The best part was a list of Top Ten Tips for Tip-Top Photos.

"Keep your camera handy at all times," read tip number ten. "The best shots can come up at surprising moments."

Jenny folded up the booklet. She grabbed her camera. She ran downstairs and headed for the front door.

"Where are you going?" her mother asked.

"Outside," said Jenny. "To wait for a surprising moment."

Jenny walked up Lemon Street toward her friend Beth's house. She looked carefully at all the houses she passed. But nothing surprising happened.

Mrs. Katz was standing at the corner of Lemon Street. Kiss-Kiss, her small dog, was dashing around her legs.

Kiss-Kiss was really Mr. Katz's dog. Mrs. Katz didn't like her very much. She was always yelling at her or complaining about her. But she had to walk her a lot.

This might be a surprising moment, Jenny thought. She hurried toward the corner.

"Stop it, Kiss-Kiss!" yelled Mrs. Katz. "*No!*"

Kiss-Kiss had twisted her leash around Mrs. Katz's legs.

This would make a funny *candied* picture, thought Jenny. She giggled to herself. She raised the camera.

"I am really fed up with you!" Mrs. Katz shouted. She bent over. She stuck her face in front of Kiss-Kiss's nose. "You're nothing but trouble, you nasty little mutt!"

She reached for the dog's collar. "Ooh, I'm going to —"

"Click!" Jenny snapped the picture just before Mrs. Katz straightened up. "Got it!"

Mrs. Katz turned around. "What are you doing?" she yelled.

"Just taking a picture," said Jenny.

Mrs. Katz started toward her. "Who said you could take my picture?"

Kiss-Kiss plopped down on the sidewalk. She wouldn't budge. Mrs. Katz yanked at her leash.

"I want that film!" she yelled. "You had no right! Come back here!"

But Jenny was so scared, she was already

across the street. She ran up the steps to Beth's house. She pounded on the front door.

"Beth! Let me in!"

The door opened. "What's the matter?" Beth asked.

Jenny pushed inside and slammed the door shut. She raced upstairs to Beth's room. Her friend hurried after her.

"Mrs. Katz is after me!" Jenny flopped onto the bed, panting.

"Why?" asked Beth.

Jenny tried to catch her breath. "Because I saw her. I saw her trying to kill Kiss-Kiss."

5

Beth's eyes grew wide as Jenny told her what had happened.

"She was grabbing Kiss-Kiss's collar," Jenny said. "Like she was going to choke her."

"Do you really think Mrs. Katz would do something like that?" said Beth.

"Why else would she not want me to take her picture?" Jenny said. "I caught her in the act."

"I know she doesn't like Kiss-Kiss," Beth said. "But I can't believe she'd hurt a helpless little dog."

"I *saw* her," said Jenny. "I think we ought to tell Mr. Katz."

"But what if you're wrong?" said Beth. "Mrs. Katz will be really mad. She might even sue you."

"That's true," said Jenny. "But what if I'm right?" She shivered. "Poor little Kiss-Kiss."

She looked out the window. Mrs. Katz was gone.

"I've got it!" Jenny said. "A letter. We can send Mr. Katz a letter. We'll warn him about Mrs. Katz. And if we don't sign it —"

"Mrs. Katz can't sue you," finished Beth. "That's a great idea!" She got a piece of paper and an envelope from her desk.

Jenny sat down and began to write.

Dear Mr. Katz,

Your dog is in danger. Your wife does not like her. She is trying to get rid of her. Please do not leave Mrs. Katz alone with Kiss-Kiss. Not even for one minute!

Sincerely,

A Worried Animal Lover

She addressed the envelope and put a stamp on it. They walked to the mailbox on the corner. Beth dropped the letter inside.

"Mr. Katz should get the letter Tuesday," said Jenny. "I hope Kiss-Kiss will be safe until then."

"The picture!" Beth said. "You took her picture."

"Of course," said Jenny. "That's how this all started."

"But it's proof!" Beth said excitedly. "Mrs. Katz can't do anything to Kiss-Kiss now. She knows you have that picture."

"That's right!" said Jenny. "Kiss-Kiss will be safe as long as I have the photo."

Beth gulped. "Kiss-Kiss will be safe," she said. "But *you* might not be."

6

Jenny's parents did not believe that Mrs. Katz wanted to kill Kiss-Kiss.

They did not believe that Jenny was in danger because of her photo.

But Jenny wouldn't even walk to her friend Wilson's house alone. Even though it was only a block away.

"All right, all right," her father said finally. "I'll walk you to Wilson's house. But you're really letting your imagination run away with you."

At Wilson's, Jenny told her friend about Mrs. Katz. She told him about the photo contest.

"Did you think of a title for Mrs. Katz's picture?" he asked.

Jenny shivered. "I don't want to think of a title for that picture. It's too awful. I wouldn't enter that photo in the contest."

"What picture will you send in?" asked Wilson.

"I haven't got any good ones yet," Jenny answered. "I haven't been outside since this morning. Mrs. Katz might be watching for me."

"I'll go out with you," Wilson said. "You can look for good pictures, and I can look out for Mrs. Katz."

Jenny thought about it. She nodded. "That should be safe," she said. "Mrs. Katz wouldn't do anything to me in front of a witness."

They went outside and walked around the corner.

"There's something surprising." Wilson pointed to Mr. Munch's driveway. "Mr. Munch has a blanket over his car."

They walked up the driveway.

"It's not a blanket," said Jenny. "It's a plastic cover. I wonder why Mr. Munch put a plastic cover over his car?"

"To keep the snow off it?" Wilson guessed.

"In May?" said Jenny. "There isn't any snow in May."

"Then why did he put a cover on his car?" asked Wilson.

"I don't know," said Jenny. "This is very mysterious."

"Maybe there isn't really a car under it," Wilson said.

"But what else could it be?"

"I don't know," said Wilson. "But I'll find out." He looked around carefully. Then he tiptoed up the driveway. He bent down. He started to lift the edge of the plastic.

This might make a good photo, thought

Jenny. A picture of Wilson looking surprised by what he sees. I could call it *Undercover Investigator.*

She raised the camera to her eye. She aimed it at Wilson.

Just then she heard a car engine. She turned her head. A car pulled into Mr. Munch's driveway, right behind Wilson.

Wilson jumped. He dropped the edge of the plastic cover. Mr. Munch got out of the car.

"What are you kids doing?" he asked.

"I have a new camera." Jenny held it out for him to see. "I'm trying to find interesting things to take pictures of."

"Did you take a picture of that?" Mr. Munch pointed to his driveway.

"I was really taking a picture of Wilson," began Jenny.

"But is that car in the picture?" Mr. Munch cut in.

So it was a car, Jenny thought. Not anything mysterious.

"Well, I didn't really —"

"Jenny, please don't show anyone that picture," Mr. Munch said. "It's very important."

"But —"

"And please don't tell anyone about this. It's a secret."

"Okay," said Jenny. "But how can it be a secret if it's right here in your driveway?"

Mr. Munch grinned. "It won't be here for long," he said. "Now promise not to show anyone that picture."

"There isn't any picture," said Jenny. "I didn't get a chance to take it."

Mr. Munch let out a deep breath. "Oh, good," he said. "Then there's nothing to worry about."

7

Jenny wondered about Mr. Munch all the way back to Wilson's house.

"Why didn't he want me to take a picture of that car?" she asked.

"I don't know," said Wilson. "It was just a plain car."

"But he's got it covered up," she said. "So no one can see it. And he doesn't want anybody to know about it. And why won't it stay in his driveway very long?"

Wilson shook his head. "It's very mysterious," he said.

"You know what I'm starting to think?" Jenny said slowly. "Maybe Mr. Munch stole that car."

"Mr. Munch?" said Wilson. "But he's so nice. Mr. Munch couldn't be a car thief."

"Did you see what kind of a car it was?" Jenny asked. "Did it look like a big, expensive one?"

"I only got a little look at the back," said Wilson. "All I could see was that it didn't have a license plate."

"It didn't have a license plate?" Jenny said.

Wilson's mouth dropped open. He was the perfect picture of surprise. But Jenny was too shocked to think of taking pictures.

"Yikes!"

"What should we do?" Wilson asked a little while later. They were in his room. "Should we tell somebody?"

Jenny twisted a strand of hair around her finger. "I'd really hate to tell on Mr. Munch," she said. "He has a wife and a baby. And a wonderful dog."

"But what if he gets arrested?" said Wilson. "What will happen to his wife and baby and dog?"

"I know!" Jenny pushed her glasses back on her nose. "We can write him a letter. Like we did with Mrs. Katz."

"That's a good idea." Wilson nodded. "We can warn him that he's being watched."

"And then he'll be afraid to steal any more cars," said Jenny. "Isn't this wonderful, Wilson? We're saving Mr. Munch from a life of crime!"

Dear Mr. Munch,

Please do not steal any more cars.

It would be terrible for your wife and baby and dog if you had to go to jail.

Remember: crime does not pay!

Sincerely,

A Worried Friend

8

Jenny was brushing her teeth the next morning when she heard her mother shout, "Oh, no! Not again!"

"Wha' ish it?" called Jenny with her mouth full of toothpaste.

"The raccoons got into the garbage," her mother called back.

"Don't clean it up!" yelled Jenny.

She wiped her mouth. She ran to get her camera. She dashed downstairs.

Her father was reaching under the sink for a trash bag.

"I'll clean it up," Jenny said. "But let me take a picture of it first."

"You want to take a picture of garbage?" her father asked.

"It's not just garbage," said Jenny. "It's raccoon garbage. And I can give it an interesting title."

"*Why I Hate Raccoons* is a good title," her mother said.

"Well, at least garbage isn't dangerous," said Jenny. "Like Mrs. Katz and Mr. Munch."

Mrs. Archer rolled her eyes. "Mrs. Katz is not dangerous."

"And what's this about Mr. Munch?" her father asked.

"Oh, never mind," said Jenny. "You'd just say I was imagining things."

"And you probably would be," said her father. He handed her the trash bag.

Outside, Jenny saw what the raccoons had done. The yard was littered with orange peels, coffee grinds, and chicken bones.

There were crumpled tissues, apple cores, and empty milk cartons. Torn envelopes, cereal boxes, and used plastic bags.

"Yuck!" she said happily. "What a mess!"

She moved around the garbage, aiming her camera. She tried shots from different angles. From any angle, the yard looked disgusting.

I'll bet no one else in the contest will have a picture of garbage, she thought. And if I can think up a clever title . . .

She put the camera down on the back steps. She pulled open the trash bag. She began to work on clever titles for her garbage picture.

Revenge of the Raccoons, she thought. *Wildlife in the Suburbs. Nightmare on Lemon Street.*

She giggled.

But suddenly she saw something that made her stop giggling.

It was a little booklet with a picture of a baby on the cover. Printed on the top in pink letters was WHAT TO NAME YOUR BABY.

Jenny was astonished. For a moment she couldn't move a muscle. Then she bent down and picked up the book. It was damp and had coffee stains on it.

She was so thrilled, she could hardly breathe.

We're going to have a baby! she thought. At last, I'm going to be a sister!

9

Jenny could hardly wait to meet Beth and Wilson on the corner.

"My mother's going to have a baby!" she shouted the moment she saw them.

"That's wonderful!" said Beth. "When?"

"I don't know," said Jenny. "It's a secret." She closed her eyes tightly and crossed her fingers. "I hope it's a girl."

"Didn't you ask?" said Wilson.

Jenny explained how she had found the baby name book. "They don't want me to know yet. So I didn't tell them I found out."

"But why wouldn't they want you to know?" asked Beth.

"There must be a good reason," said Jenny. "But I hope they tell me soon. It's *really* hard pretending not to know."

Jenny couldn't keep her mind on schoolwork that day. All she could think about was her baby sister. She started making a list of names in her notebook.

Melissa. Jacqueline. Betsy. Felicity.

Felicity Archer. What a beautiful name! Jenny underlined it three times.

What if it's a boy? she thought. Maybe I should plan some boys' names.

She wrote down Michael and Max and Rock. But boys' names were so boring.

She started listing silly names. Marmaduke and Dweezil and Buford.

She closed her eyes and crossed her fingers.

It's just *got* to be a little sister.

* * *

When Jenny got home from school, Mrs. Butterfield was waiting for her. Mrs. Butterfield stayed with Jenny while her parents were at work.

"Mrs. Katz was looking for you," Mrs. Butterfield said.

"Uh-oh." Jenny gulped. Mrs. Katz must have gotten hold of her letter.

"She seemed angry," Mrs. Butterfield said.

"Uh-oh."

"And someone named Mr. Munch called," Mrs. Butterfield said. "He sounded upset, too."

"Uh-oh." Mr. Munch must have figured out who his letter was from.

Mrs. Butterfield looked at her sharply. "Can't you say something besides uh-oh?"

"Yikes," Jenny whispered.

The Archers were just starting dinner when the doorbell rang.

"What timing," groaned her father. He put down his fork.

"Don't answer it," Jenny said. "Our food will get cold."

Mrs. Archer stared at her. "Jenny, it's tuna macaroni salad. It's already cold."

"Then we don't want it to get warm," Jenny said.

The doorbell rang again. Barkley ran to the door, barking. He ran back to the kitchen. He barked at Mr. Archer.

"I'm coming, I'm coming!" Jenny's father shouted. He looked over at Jenny. "Why don't you want me to answer the door?" he asked.

"No reason," said Jenny, and crawled under the table.

Her mother leaned down and peered at her. "Jenny, what in the world is going on?"

But before she could answer, they heard screaming in the living room.

10

Jenny could make out only a few words.

"This letter! . . . Hurt the dog! . . . I should sue you!"

Mrs. Archer hurried out of the kitchen. Jenny stayed under the table.

But not for long.

"Jenny! Come in here!" her father yelled.

Jenny crawled out from under the table. Very slowly. She told herself that Mrs. Katz couldn't hurt her. Not with her parents right there.

But she was still scared.

She walked into the living room. Very slowly.

Her father was holding a piece of paper. Her mother was reading it over his shoulder.

Mrs. Katz's face was bright red.

"Did you write this letter, Jenny?" her father asked. He held out the paper for her to look at.

She nodded.

"Why would you do something like that?" asked her mother.

"I told you," answered Jenny. "But you didn't believe me. I saw her trying to choke Kiss-Kiss."

"How can you say such a thing?" shrieked Mrs. Katz. "How could you *write* such a thing?"

Barkley placed himself between Jenny and Mrs. Katz. Jenny felt a little braver with Barkley protecting her.

"I have proof," Jenny said. "I took a picture.

And you were mad at me because I caught you in the act."

"Caught me in the — I wasn't mad because you — where is that picture?" Mrs. Katz sputtered.

"It's still in the camera," Jenny said. "I didn't get it developed yet."

"Oh, my goodness!" said Jenny's mother. "I completely forgot. I found the camera on the back steps. All the shots were used up. So I took it into the photo shop this morning."

She went to get her pocketbook. "I got the pictures on my way home," she said.

"I demand to have that picture!" Mrs. Katz said loudly. "You're not even to *look* at it!"

"See?" said Jenny. "That's proof! She doesn't want us to see —"

The doorbell rang.

Mrs. Katz was still shouting as Mr. Archer went to answer it.

Mr. Munch and his wife stood on the doorstep. Mrs. Munch was holding their baby. Mr. Munch was holding a piece of paper. He handed it to Jenny's father.

"Another letter?" Mr. Archer said. "Jenny, what's gotten into you?"

For a moment nobody said anything. Not even Mrs. Katz.

"You always seemed so nice," Jenny told Mr. Munch. "I didn't want you to start on a life of crime."

"Where did you get that idea?" asked Mr. Munch.

"The car you stole. In your driveway." Jenny was not nearly as scared of Mr. Munch as she was of Mrs. Katz.

"It had a plastic cover to hide it. And no license plate."

"I didn't steal it," Mr. Munch said. "I told you, it was a surprise. At least, it was supposed to be a surprise. Till you ruined it."

"But you said it wasn't going to be in your

driveway long," Jenny reminded him. "And it didn't have a license plate. And you made me promise not to tell anyone about it."

"Because it was a surprise for Carol," he said. "I got it while she was away."

"Visiting my mother," said Mrs. Munch.

"And I was going to keep it at a friend's house," Mr. Munch went on. "Until her birthday."

"Today," said Mrs. Munch.

"And there was no license plate because I hadn't gotten one yet."

"Oh," said Jenny.

"And if you took a picture, you might have shown it to me," said Mrs. Munch. "Before my birthday."

"Oh," said Jenny.

"When your letter came, marked *urgent,* Carol called me at work," said Mr. Munch. "Naturally I told her to open it."

"Uh-oh," said Jenny.

Mr. Munch glared at her. "So instead of surprising her on her birthday with a new car, I have to explain why I'm not a car thief."

Mrs. Archer folded her arms across her chest. She gave Jenny a long, hard look. "I think you have something to say to Mr. and Mrs. Munch. Don't you, Jenny?"

Jenny looked at Mrs. Munch. She tried to smile.

"Happy birthday?"

11

"What about my photo?" roared Mrs. Katz.

Barkley yelped. The Munches' baby woke up and started to cry.

"Oh, yes," said Mrs. Archer. "I have the pictures right here." She handed the packet of photos to Mrs. Katz.

"Ask her why she doesn't want us to see them," Jenny whispered.

"Jenny, I don't want to hear one more word from you," her mother warned.

Jenny's father turned to the Munches.

"We're really sorry about this," he said. "And I'm sure Jenny will apologize when she's allowed to talk again."

Jenny looked down at her feet. She was glad her mother wouldn't let her say anything. She wouldn't know what to say to Mr. Munch.

But that didn't mean she was wrong about Mrs. Katz.

"Here it is!" Mrs. Katz pulled a photo from the pack. She dropped the rest of the pictures on the coffee table. She looked at the photo. Her cheeks grew even redder.

"I hope you will talk to this child about writing poison pen letters." She scowled at Jenny and stuck the photo into her sweater pocket. "And about taking pictures of people who don't want their pictures taken."

"We will," said Jenny's mother.

"And calling people thieves," said Mr. Munch. "Without any proof."

"She has a powerful imagination," Jenny's father said.

SPEEDY
PHOTO

"She needs a powerful spanking!" said Mrs. Katz.

"She *needs* — a quiet talk," Mr. Archer said. "About the difference between imagination and facts."

"And you can be sure we'll have that talk," said Mrs. Archer. "The moment you leave." She gave Jenny a stern look.

Jenny felt like hiding behind the sofa. She had never been so embarrassed in her life. The way they were talking about her! As if she were three years old. As if she weren't even there.

When everybody left, her parents started yelling.

"You said we'd have a quiet talk!" Jenny cried. "This isn't a quiet talk!"

"We'll talk quietly when we're finished yelling!" yelled her father.

"I'll never write another letter to anyone!" Jenny promised. "I'll never suspect anybody of anything ever again. I'll never even take another picture! Except for the new baby."

"New baby?" Jenny's parents stopped yelling.

"What new baby?"

Jenny hadn't meant to let on that she knew. But maybe it was just as well. At least her parents had stopped yelling.

"I know you wanted it to be a secret," she said. "I found out by accident."

"What are you talking about?" asked her mother.

"I saw the baby name book," said Jenny. "When I was taking pictures of the garbage. Did you pick a name yet? I have some ideas."

Jenny's mother looked confused. "A name for *what*?"

"For the baby," Jenny said.

"I did pick a name," her mother said. "It was Jenny."

"But that's *my* name. I mean a name for the new baby."

"Wait a minute," said Mrs. Archer. She rubbed her forehead. "You saw a book in the garbage? And decided I was going to have a baby?"

"Aren't you?" asked Jenny.

"No," said Mrs. Archer. "I was cleaning out my closet. I found the book with a bunch of other junk. It must be ten years old."

"Ohhh." Jenny flopped onto the sofa. She put her head in her hands.

She'd spoiled Mrs. Munch's birthday. Mr. Munch would probably never speak to her again. Mrs. Katz wanted her spanked.

Her parents were furious at her.

And she wasn't going to have a baby sister.

What a terrible day.

12

"Let me get this straight," her father said. "In the last three days, you decided Mrs. Katz was a dog killer. Mr. Munch was a car thief. And your mother was going to have a baby."

"Well . . . ," said Jenny.

"And you were wrong about all three," her father said.

"We still don't know about Mrs. Katz," Jenny said stubbornly. "She never let us see her picture."

"Jenny!" her father yelled. "Haven't you learned *anything*?"

"I have an extra copy!" her mother said suddenly. "The photo store gave me double prints!"

Jenny leapt off the sofa. Mrs. Katz had dropped the packet of photos on the coffee table. Jenny picked eagerly through the pictures.

"Here it is!" Jenny looked at the photo. "See, there's Mrs. Katz bending over and — oh."

Her mother looked at the photo. "No wonder Mrs. Katz didn't want us to see it." She showed the picture to Jenny's father.

He took one look at it. Then he handed it back to Jenny. "This is not a picture of a woman choking a dog," he said.

"No," Jenny said softly. She looked at the photo again.

It was very clear. Mrs. Katz, bent over Kiss-Kiss. And a long rip, right up the seat of her green slacks.

"I didn't see that in the camera," Jenny said.

"You saw a lot of other things," her mother said. "Things that weren't there."

"I guess my imagination did run away with me," Jenny said. "A lot."

"Your imagination can do whatever it wants," her father said. "But you can't accuse people of things without real proof."

"I thought the picture was real proof," Jenny said.

"But now you know it wasn't," her mother said.

"And when you don't sign your name," said her father, "that's even worse."

"Is that what 'poison pen letter' means?" asked Jenny.

Her father nodded. "If you don't sign your name, then people don't know who's saying bad things about them. So they can't defend themselves."

Jenny sighed. "I guess I won't be writing any more letters," she said. "And I don't think I'm going to be taking any more pictures, either. They both got me in trouble."

"You've still got time to enter the contest," her mother said. She was flipping through the rest of the photos. "These are a lot better than your first batch."

"Are they really?" Jenny picked up one of

the pictures. "This is a good shot of the garbage," she said. "You can even see the baby name book."

Her eyes lit up. "You know, if I had a baby sister, I would never get in trouble."

"Why not?" her father asked.

"I'd be too busy taking care of her," said Jenny. "I wouldn't have time to use my imagination."

Her father laughed. "You'd find time, Jenny," he said. "Somehow, you'd find the time."